DARK CLAW

Rat Trap

May the Guiding Paw be with you!

Shoo Rayner

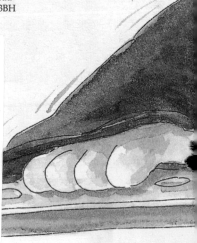

Chapter 1

Dark Claw paced the control room of
his secret space station, Dark Moon.
He banged the control desk with
his fist. "I will have r-evenge!"
he snarled.

Revenge!

The small gang of Pi-rats in front of
him shuddered.

"You have failed me once,"
Dark Claw growled at them.
"You will not fail me again."

"N-n-n-no! D-d-d-dark Claw," stammered Ratuschka, the Pi-rat leader.

Of course not!

Dark Claw's one mission in life was to rid the universe of all living Muss. But there was one Muss he wanted to destroy above all others... Onlee One.

For though he was still at school, Onlee One had already upset Dark Claw's evil plans.
Not once, but twice…

This time Dark Claw would see to it that the interfering Muss would be silenced, once and for all.

Dark Claw handed something to Ratuschka. She examined it closely.

It was a small, grey box with a stubby funnel on top. Ratuschka waited for Dark Claw to explain.

"It's a smell repeater. My Robodroids are fitting hundreds of these devices on the surface of Dark Moon," he told her.

Ratuschka looked confused, so
Dark Claw continued.

Muss use their
excellent sense of smell to
navigate through space. Their
Nosar systems are so sensitive,
they can even smell Dark Moon.
We are not safe.

Dark Claw smiled. He liked to show how clever he was. He drew a diagram of how it all worked.

These pick up a smell from one side of Dark Moon and send it out again on the other. The smell of Dark Moon stays where it is.

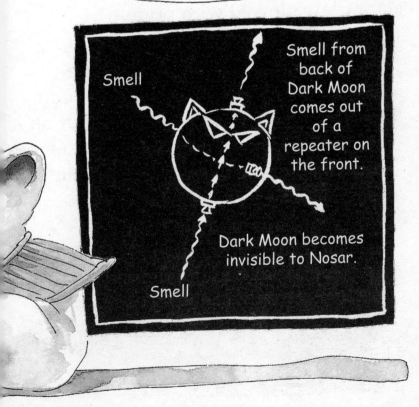

Smell

Smell from back of Dark Moon comes out of a repeater on the front.

Dark Moon becomes invisible to Nosar.

Smell

Ratuschka's eyes opened wide.
She understood what it meant.

Dark Moon
will be invisible
to the Muss!

Dark Claw glowed with pride.

Precisely! Once we
are invisible we can begin
the master plan, to put an
end to the Muss race and
Onlee One in particular.

With Dark Claw in such a good mood, Ratuschka dared to ask him something she'd always wanted to know.

Straight away she wished she hadn't asked. Dark Claw fixed her with a stare that turned her blood to ice.

"That is my business!" he hissed through clenched teeth.

Chapter 2

In the Year Five study at the Tan Monastery School, Hammee was making more toast.

"There's hardly room to butter a sandwich in here," he complained.

> So many trophies and medals! I think it's time you retired, Onlee One!

Onlee One rolled his eyes.
He, Hammee and Chin Chee were prize-winning tunnel-mazers.
As well as trophies, they often won huge pieces of cheese, Hammee's favourite! He couldn't *really* want Onlee One to retire!

Still, the huge collection of trophies set Onlee One thinking. He looked at his friend Chin Chee.

Chin Chee smiled. There *was* something special – something different – about Onlee One.

Onlee One was an orphan. He had arrived at the Monastery as a baby, not knowing who his parents were. All he knew was that he had a special gift – an amazing sense of smell! Now, more than ever, Onlee One wanted to know about his past.

As they lined up for supper that night, Onlee One stared at a painting on the wall. It was a portrait of Pale One, the school's most famous "old boy".

"He's always been my hero," said Onlee One.

The other two said nothing. It was best to keep quiet when he was in one of these moods.

Onlee One and Pale One shared the same name. But that didn't have to mean anything ... did it?

Onlee One nodded.
"I've made up my mind," he said.

I'm going to
see the Abbot
after supper.
I'm going to ask him
who I am!

Chapter 3

All the Monastery orphans went to Abbot Grey when they were old enough to find out who their parents were. If anyone could tell them, he could.

The kind old Muss smiled at Onlee One.

It's time you knew how you came to be given to the Monastery. Wait here, there is someone I'd like you to meet.

A few minutes later, Abbot Grey
returned with the school cook.

He put his hands on the cook's
shoulders and smiled at Onlee One.

This... is your mother!

Onlee One's neck hairs stood on end.
A thrill swept through his body.
His ears twitched out of control.
He couldn't help it.

"Mother!?"
Onlee One gasped.

"My little boy!"
said the cook.
Her eyes were
wet with tears.

Chapter 4

Abbot Grey left the two alone.

Onlee One's mother smiled.
"There must be a million questions you
want to ask me," she said.

But Onlee One was lost for words.

Looking into her eyes he suddenly saw his own. The same colour, the same shape. It was true! She really was his mother. He threw himself into her arms and cried like a baby…

… he couldn't help it!

She held him close.

After a long time, he broke the silence.
"If you are my mother, who is my father?"

She didn't answer straight away.
She stared out of the window, as
if she was looking for something…
or someone.

Deep in his heart Onlee One knew what she would say. When she finally spoke, her voice was choked with sadness. "Pale One was your father."

"I always knew it," he whispered.

Chapter 5

Over the next few weeks, Onlee One got to know his mother well. They spent hours looking at old photographs and talking together in her room.

Onlee One pointed to a picture of Pale One. "What's this mark on his arm?" he asked.

"That's a long story," his mother said.

Your father was sent on a mission to the Planet Kat. He became friendly with a Kat family and sometimes stayed at their home.

Sadly, he gave their baby kitten a cold. A cold is not serious for us, but the kitten became very ill. It had to spend the rest of it's life in a wheelchair.

The kitten's claws were all white, except for one, so they called it 'Dark Claw.' Your father had a dark claw tattooed on his arm so that he would never forget.

Onlee One looked at the scar on his forearm. It was exactly the same size and shape as his father's tattoo. He had been wounded by that same dark claw! Could destiny have bound Onlee One and Dark Claw together so closely?

Onlee One pointed to another photo.
It was a picture of Pale One and
another Muss.

"It is," said his mother. "They were
best friends at school. It was Brandling
who told me that your father had gone
missing on an important mission. I was
out of my mind with worry."

She blew her nose and carried on.

Your father never returned. Brandling took me to a nunnery where I hid away for years. The nuns told everyone that my baby had died. They thought it was for the best.

Eventually, I felt better, and found out that you were alive. I left the nunnery and came here, looking for you. The Abbot was very kind and gave me a job. But he would not let me tell you who I was until you were old enough. It's been very hard to keep the secret.

Chapter 6

Onlee One wrote to Chancellor Brandling. He asked if it was possible to go to the planet Kat, to find out more about his father.

A reply came quickly.
A new ambassador was leaving for Kat very soon. As Onlee One and his friends were such a famous tunnel-mazing team, they could represent the youth of Muss on the mission.

Brandling came to see them off. She was thrilled to learn that Onlee One was her old friend's son.

Before their ship left, she talked about Pale One.

The nuns told everyone you had died in childbirth. Your father took the news very badly. He went to Kat and was never heard of again. I still miss him. He was my best friend.

"I hope I can learn more about him from the Kats," said Onlee One. "I may also learn more about Dark Claw too."

Brandling nodded wisely. "Keep me informed, young One. Send me news of what you find out. We think Dark Claw may be up to his old tricks again."

"I will," said Onlee One. "And thank you for making this trip possible."

Brandling bowed her head slightly. "Anything for the son of my dearest old friend, Pale One."

Chapter 7

Everything on the planet Kat was a bit bigger than it was on the planet Muss – because Kats are bigger than Muss!

Onlee One, Hammee and Chin Chee were curious about this strange new planet they were on.

"This stew is an interesting colour," said Hammee. "What's in it?"

"Toad Brains!" said their host.

Hammee turned green.
Suddenly he felt sick.

"Actually," their host said with a smile, "they're not really toad's brains, they just look like them. They're really a sort of dumpling."

Hammee sighed with relief.

The three friends travelled the planet showing off their skills at tunnel-mazing.

Tunnel Mazing Exhibition

At the end of the trip they were invited
to meet Top Kat for an official dinner.
He was the leader of the Kats and a
little bit scary.

"So, you are the son of Pale One!"
he boomed at Onlee One.
"We remember him well."

"You knew my father?" Onlee One was amazed. I was hoping to find out more about him while I was here."

The Kat Leader smiled at him.
"We knew you were coming so we did some checking. We think he went to the planet Libera with the Purrley family."

Top Kat told him that Libera was near the planet Felicity. In the bad old days, the Muss and the Kats had fought over Felicity and destroyed it.

It had been a green and beautiful planet, now it was just a frozen desert. The Kats and Muss were so shocked by what they had done, they made peace with each other.

Some Kats and Muss
had gone to Libera to learn to live
together in peace and harmony.

Onlee One felt a question burning
inside him.

Did the Purrley family
have a kitten called Dark
Claw?

Top Kat's eyes narrowed.

Dark Claw was a very clever kitten. He built a robo-suit and freed himself from his wheelchair. He then built his army of Robo Kats, but was caught and sent into exile. He is now a very dangerous Kat, but no one knows where he is.

Chapter 8

On the journey home, Onlee One went to the control room. He sent a message to Brandling, telling her what he had found out about his father and Dark Claw.

The captain was showing him the controls. He was pointing out their position on the Nosar screen when something hit the side of the ship.

"We're under attack!" the pilot shouted.

"We can't be!" said the captain pointing at the Nosar screen.

There's nothing there.

"Kerrang!" something else hit them hard. On the view screen, a Pi-rat ship shot past them, lasers blazing.

"Red alert!" yelled the captain. "Return fire!"

Alarms sounded throughout the ship.

Onlee One's heart thumped like a drum. This couldn't be happening. He recognised the Pi-rat ship. He had once captured and flown it himself!

"Ratuschka!" he hissed to himself.

That means Dark Claw can't be far away!

rring!

The floor shook as their massive laser cannons fired in defence. The Pi-rat ship turned and fled. But where to? It still didn't show up on the Nosar.

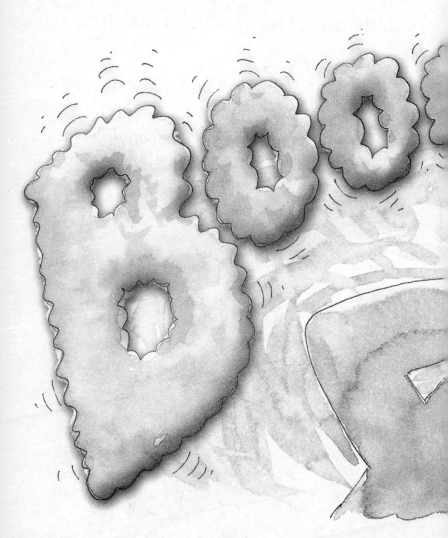

If the Pi-rats were invisible maybe Dark Claw was too. Onlee One wasted no time sending a new message to Brandling. The sooner she knew the better.

The ship was slightly damaged, but they limped home and landed safe and sound.

Hammee was impatient for some "real" home-cooked food at the spaceport. He licked his lips as the outside doors slid open.

Do Not Open During Flight

Space Doors

Keep Closed During Flight

A squad of Muss guards was waiting for them.

"Come with us!" ordered the leader.

They were taken to a small room and locked inside. The three friends sat on a bench and waited.

"This feels like a prison cell," said Chin Chee.

"And a prison cell is exactly what it is!" Brandling announced, bursting into the room with two guards.

The three young Muss couldn't believe their ears.

Brandling bared her teeth. It wasn't a smile, more a horrible, cold grimace. "You will be charged with treason in the morning," she snarled.

Then, as quickly as she had come, she was gone.

The door slammed shut behind her.

Chapter 9

Invisible to the Muss, Dark Claw
watched the latest Seekah spy reports.
He turned to his Pi-rat helpers.

Well done! Your little run-in with the Muss has done the trick. The master-plan is working. Revenge will be mine, my friends. Revenge will be mine!

Have you seen the Dark Claw Website?

www.dark-claw.co.uk

Shoo Rayner designed and built the Dark Claw Website himself, while he was writing the Dark Claw stories. It is packed full of games and background stories about the worlds of Onlee One, his friends and his enemies!

Why is Dark Claw so angry?
Why does he want to destroy the Muss?

 Where in the Universe is the planet Muss?
What is Litterbox? What is Kimono?

What is it like at the Tan Monastery School?
Why do the beds squeak?

All this and more. If you're a Dark Claw fan, you'll love the Dark Claw website. It's all part of the story!

If you enjoyed this book you'll want to read the other books in the Dark Claw Saga.

Tunnel Mazers
0 340 81754 2
The one with the very
smelly cheese!

Road Rage
0 340 81755 0
The one with the cool
racing machines!

Rat Trap
0 340 81756 9
The one with invisible
space ships!

Breakout!
0 340 81757 7
The one with nowhere
left to go!

The Guiding Paw
0 340 81758 5
The one with the Muss-
eating jellyfish!

The Black Hole
0 340 81759 3
The one with the end
of the story!

Find out more about Shoo Rayner and his other
fantastic books at www.shoo-rayner.co.uk

If you enjoyed this book you'll love these other books by Shoo Rayner and Hodder Children's Books

The Rex Files
(Seriously weird!)

0 340 71432 8	The Life-Snatcher
0 340 71466 2	The Phantom Bantam
0 340 71467 0	The Bermuda Triangle
0 340 71468 9	The Shredder
0 340 71469 7	The Frightened Forest
0 340 71470 0	The Baa-Baa Club

Or what about the wonderful
Ginger Ninja?

0 340 61955 4	The Ginger Ninja
0 340 61956 2	The Return of Tiddles
0 340 61957 0	The Dance of the Apple Dumplings
0 340 61958 9	St Felix for the Cup
0 340 69379 7	World Cup Winners
0 340 69380 0	Three's a Crowd

And don't forget SUPERDAD!
(He's a bit soft really!)

0 7500 2694 4	Superdad
0 7500 2706 1	Superdad the SuperHero